So I'n

SO I'M ON A BUS

SIOAB1

Mikey Glenister

Written by Mikey Glenister

Illustrations, Design & Artwork by Lee Baker
leebs69@hotmail.com

Printed and Bound by Cambrian Printers, UK

A catologue copy is available from the British Library

ISBN 9781910399002

© Zeshan Qureshi 2015

So I'm on a Bus...

by
Mikey Glenister

illustrated by Lee Baker

So I'm on a bus. As always, I show the driver my bus pass.

He looks at me and says, "That's expired."

I tell him that it isn't.

He angrily raises his voice and says, "You're the fourth person already this morning to try this stunt. Do you think I'm stupid? I don't have 'mug' written on my forehead. Pay for where you're going or get off my bus!"

With the whole bus looking on, I politely say, "It's the second today. My pass expires on the third."

The driver's transition from angry to embarrassed is quite the sight. Especially when the passengers cheer as he lets me on.

So I'm on a bus. The biggest woman I've ever seen is sitting next to me. There were empty double seats available when she sat down ten minutes ago.

I wouldn't normally pass judgement, but she's already on her third bag of prawn cocktail crisps.

Please don't eat me.

So I'm on a bus. The back of the bus to be precise. No cool school kids in sight, though. In a bizarre reversal to the norm (insufferable brats and chavs), geeks rule the roost. And boy, don't they know it. They are embracing this rare occurrence.

We have three young chaps, happily solving quadratic equations for fun; pompous and loud in their competitive nature, but all incapable of working out the basic mechanics of how to wear a necktie.

We have an odd-looking fellow talking to himself, drawing a work of art on the steamed-up windows, whilst the token fat kid looks on, eating his packed lunch of pungent garlic sausage sandwiches.

And finally we have four bespectacled gentlemen talking extensively about cracked Halo maps, Minecraft creations and advanced Call of Duty tactics, each trying to outdo the other with their accomplishments. The loudest of the four is so passionate about how incredible he is that he's blissfully unaware he has half a tube of toothpaste smeared across his cheek.

Today, geek is cool.

So I'm on a bus. A mother's young son is shouting, "Mum! Mum! Mum! Mum!" whilst she is talking to her friend. He's incredibly persistent.

She suddenly decides she's had enough, turns around to him and shouts, "Son! Son! Son! Son!"

He stops. Clearly he doesn't like this.

"Not very nice, is it?" she says to him.

Then he punches her in the face.

10

So I'm on a bus. It's New Year's Eve, and a group of boozed-up girls press the stop button and stand ready to get off the bus. As one of them walks past me, her bag brushes my head. I look up, to be greeted by the sight of her wearing a pair of hot pants that are two sizes too small, with her bottom struggling to stay inside its tiny constraints. I honestly don't know where to look, a thought that's also shared by a pack of horny teenage boys, hypnotised by her divine buttocks as they pass.

Suddenly the girl turns round to me and dramatically asks me, "Are you looking at my bum?"

"Well, yes. I am," I reply. "The *whole bus* is looking at your bum."

She looks at me, rather startled at my response.

"We don't really have a choice," I continue, "there's more bum cheek than hot pant there, my dear. But I'm sure that was the look you were going for, so don't fret about it. You've totally nailed it. Happy New Year!"

"Um, Happy New Year," she says coyly, as the bus stops and her and her friends step out into the icy cold rain. The horny boys start laughing, but I'm just concerned that she'll freeze and be stuck in those hot pants forever.

So I'm running for a bus. The bus driver can see me sticking my arm out as I run straight towards him. He just looks at me and drives out of the station.

Not impressed.

I look at the bus timetable to see when the next bus is due, only to find that the bus I was running for left three minutes early. He had loads of time to stop and let me on.

Again, not impressed.

I see the bus stuck in a fair bit of slow moving traffic ahead. I'm running late; I need to get this bus. Knowing that the bus route weaves around a busy high street, I rashly decide to make a run for the next bus stop via a shortcut that includes an incredibly steep hill.

After a three-minute sprint, I make it to my bus stop, drained, out of breath and dripping with sweat. A minute later, my bus pulls up. I step on, still an absolute state.

"You okay, son?" the driver says chirpily.

"No, I'm not really," I explain, "You must have seen me running for your bus, but rather than wait for me, you drove off *three minutes* earlier than the time dictated on the bus timetable. So I just ran up that big bastard hill to get my bus. So thanks for that. Single to Kenneth Road please."

The bus driver looks at me as I rummage for change, and says "Cracking effort, son. On you get" gesturing me on to his bus.

I sit down with a warped sense of accomplishment and a massive urge to throw up from exhaustion.

13

So I'm on a bus. We stop at a red light. Naturally, as it's Halloween, five hooded youths loitering outside a general store proceed to bombard the bus with dozens of eggs. Some elderly passengers look on at the young hooligans disapprovingly, who are laughing away at their ridiculous exploits.

Then the shop owner comes out of the store and chucks a bucket of water over them. They are drenched. It's awesome.

It's a real shame that the lights turn green. I would love to see the fallout from this volatile situation.

So I'm at a bus stop. An old aged pensioner asks me if I know when her next bus is due. Knowing that this will inevitably lead to her trying to start small talk (you know the sort: lonely oldies who will bombard you with their life stories as soon as you throw any acknowledgement their way), I reluctantly tell her.

Sure enough, she starts talking to me like I'm her only friend in the world. She won't stop talking. She's barely stopping for breath. I give her one-word answers hoping that she'll get the hint. It's far too early for small talk, and I'm far too grumpy for human interaction.

Then she says, "So how have you been, Michael? How's your mum getting on? It's your birthday soon, isn't it?"

Crap. So I'm meant to know this lady. I don't recognise her at all. Now I have to humour her.

Thankfully her bus turns up.

"Send my love to your family. Have a lovely day!"

Either I don't recognise my friends and family and I'm going to hell, or I have an incredibly passionate elderly stalker.

Crikey.

So I'm on a bus. I'm tired, cranky and cold. My senses are heightened to the tiniest irritations. I just want to sleep for the next thirty minutes. The bus is stuck in traffic and every time it comes to a halt, the seat I'm sitting in rattles violently, shaking my entire body.

This is infuriating. I should move seats, but I don't want to be that guy – the guy that moves seats for no reason. Passengers will judge you for such a rash manoeuvre. I want to be as incognito as possible. Moving seats will draw unwanted attention to me. Such is the irrational logic of how to behave on a bus.

This rattling makes me want to smash my head against the seat in front of me. It feels like Chinese water torture. It's no good – I have to move seats. I get up and switch to the other side of the bus, with the prying, judgemental eyes of strangers fixed upon me. They must think I'm mental for moving seats. At least I've successfully got away from the insane rattling.

The bus stops again. This new seat rattles three times worse than the previous seat.

I am broken.

So I'm on a bus. I'm on my way to work, as usual. There are three teenagers at the back, being loud and lippy. They're cocky, and clearly get off on the sound of their own voices. I ignore them.

Then out of the blue, one of them comes up and says to me, "Oi, mate, you look like a twat with that ponytail."

I reply, "I'm on my way to work, and health and safety regulations require me to have my hair tied back in the workplace. What's your excuse for looking like a twat?"

Silence. Victory.

So I'm on a bus...

BUS	DESTINATION	TIME
11	Flying Low	09:53

So I'm on a bus. Just been woken up by a sweet old lady who has kindly informed me that my flies are undone.

So I'm on a bus. A mum with her pram and two young girls gets on the bus. While the mum is paying for the fares, the two children excitedly run to the back and sit right next to me.

"Hi, my name is Ashley, nice to meet you!" says one of the girls enthusiastically.

"Hi there," I say, a little bemused by the fearless openness of the girl.

"Look at my spider!" she shouts, and with that whips out a massive tarantula.

"Jesus Christ!" I exclaim, jumping out of my skin.

After realising very quickly that it was in fact a toy spider, the mother finally comes over to her girls, who are gleefully laughing their heads off.

"I'm so sorry!" she says to me apologetically. I smile and nod acceptingly as she escorts her kids back to the front of the bus.

"Put that bloody spider away. And what have I told you about talking to strangers?!"

Don't worry. I'm pretty sure I was more scared of her than she was of me.

```
┌─────────────────────────────────────────────────┐
│  So I'm on a bus...                              │
│  ───────────────────────────────────────────    │
│  BUS  DESTINATION                      TIME      │
│   13  Gives You Wings                  10:20     │
└─────────────────────────────────────────────────┘
```

So I'm on a bus. To the woman telling her screaming four-year-old to be quiet: the answer to his question, "Can I have a Red Bull now?" is not "yes."

You complete and utter moron.

So I'm on a bus. I'm standing at the front as I'm only going a couple of stops.

As the bus cuts slowly through the traffic, another bus driver is driving the other way.

As is customary, our bus driver does a wave of acknowledgement. The driver in the other bus, however, looks at him in disgust, shakes his head, and looks the other way.

I'm intrigued. What on earth could he have possibly done to cause him to break this sacred ritual of bus drivers, that's been passed down through generations?

My driver looks a broken man. It must have been really bad.

So I'm at a bus stop. Standing with three students. A young driver on the other side of the road slows down, leans out the window and shouts "BUS WANKERS!" at us, much to the amusement of his passengers.

He, of course, doesn't see that the traffic has slowed down for a red light, and proceeds to hit the car in front of him.

An elderly man gets out of the car he struck and talks to the young lad, who is being very brash and intimidating, insisting that it was the old man's fault for braking suddenly.

Sensing the gentleman was losing the argument, I pop over the road and tell the man, "If you need any witnesses, the boy was not looking where he was going when he was leaning out of his window shouting profanities at us. There are four of us standing at the bus stop over there who can back this up."

Needless to say, the correct details were exchanged.

Who's the wanker now?

So I'm on a bus...

BUS	DESTINATION	TIME
16	Christmas Spirit	18:07

So I'm on a bus. A gentleman is on the phone in front of me.

"I'm pleased you're getting into the Christmas spirit, I really am. But why does that mean you have to be a complete bastard for the other eleven months of the year?"

Good point. Well made.

So I'm on a bus. A lady has dropped her handbag and its contents are now rolling all over the moving bus. She's trying to pick everything up whilst having the most horrific argument with her other half on the phone.

I should give her a hand but she's terrifying, quite frankly. Pure rage personified.

Instead I decide that it's wiser to watch her stumble around, swearing aggressively down her phone in one hand, her other hand switching between taking her possessions off the wet, muddy floor and hanging on to poles for dear life, as the bus flies manically around corners.

It's better this way. Never poke the bear.

So I'm on a bus. An elderly man, who appears to be in his nineties, stands up to get off at the next bus stop. The bus goes over a pothole in the road, causing the old man to fall over in the aisle.

We passengers are immediately concerned and get up ready to help him to his feet, as the bus driver slows the bus down to a stop, noticing what has just happened.

Before we can get to him, the old gentleman jumps to his feet and declares, "I learnt that off Charlie Chaplin!"

What an absolute chap.

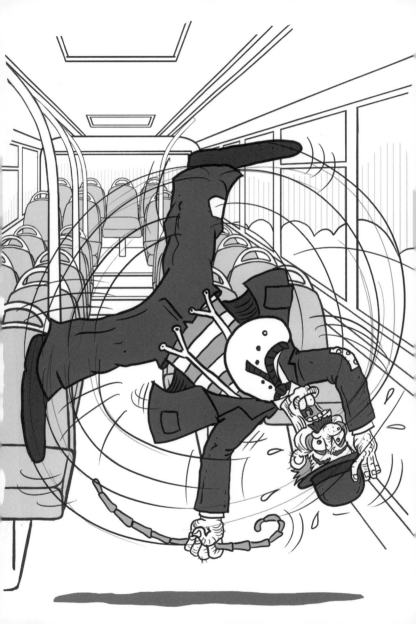

BUS	DESTINATION	TIME
19	Early Bird	07:09

So I'm on a bus. I'm sat behind a father and his daughter.

"Look, Dad! Windows! Look, Dad! Trees! Look, Dad! Leaves! Dad, we're going that way. Why aren't we going this way? My ear hurts! Can I get some water? Dad, look, more trees! Wow, we're going fast! Weeeeeee! These seats are green! There are lights on the ceiling! That man just sneezed. Atchoo, atchoo! I want to drive the bus! I'm on a bus! Aaaaaaahh! Look, more trees!"

After a couple of minutes of this from the little girl, I decide to get off the bus and get the one behind me. It's far too early for this barrage of relentless enthusiasm.

30

So I'm at a bus stop. It's absolutely pissing it down. Currently amusing me is a fairly big man holding lots of shopping, his iPhone and a pack of chocolate digestives, which he's struggling to eat due to having his hands full. As the bus appears through the fog in the distance, he panics. In doing so, he drops his iPhone, which smashes on impact with the pavement, and his digestives, which go everywhere.

Naturally, he picks up all the soggy digestives first before attending to his broken phone.

On the bus, he appears to be contemplating tucking into the dropped biscuits. He genuinely seems more gutted about the digestives than his ruined phone. I guess you can't claim for biscuits on insurance.

So I'm on a bus. There's a young couple and their three year-old daughter eating fried chicken at the back of the bus.

The couple are noisy, shouting, chucking used chicken bones everywhere, burping, swearing with their mouthfuls of food spraying everywhere, arguing and intimidating the other passengers.

The three year-old, on the other hand, has impeccable manners; sitting quietly, mouth closed whilst eating. She even neatly folds her paper napkin and places it back in her empty chicken box once she's finished.

I feel like going up to the young girl and saying, "If you're not responsible enough to control your parents, you shouldn't take them out in the first place."

So I'm on a bus. I'm sat right at the front near the driver. He is burning my ears off with his incessant talking.

Bus driver, please don't talk to me. One, I'm in a foul mood. Two, your banter is nauseating. And three, you're turning around to face me WHILST DRIVING AROUND A BLOODY CORNER.

So I'm at a bus stop. A kid is heading towards me on a scooter. He looks up to make sure he has my attention and that of the other people waiting for a bus, and proceeds to start doing some tricks. He's eager to entertain his newly-acquired audience.

The thing is, when someone does a great trick on a skateboard, it's awesome. When someone does a great trick on a BMX bike, it's awesome. When someone does a great trick on a scooter, they are still just some prick on a scooter.

35

So I'm on a bus. There's a young mother with her baby and pram. The baby is shouting quite happily.

"Ah wee wee wah wah wee wah wee wee wah wah…"

He has the biggest smile on his face. It's relentless but cute. He's having a fantastic time on the bus.

This is, however, infuriating a drunk, greasy middle-aged man sat just behind them. Armed with a trusty can of Special Brew, he's muttering curses to himself and cringing at every sound that comes out of the baby's mouth.

Soon, he's had enough and slurs, "Will you please take care of your baby? Shut him up for goodness' sake!"

The mother looks at him in disgust and says, "I'm not taking advice from someone that smells of booze and piss. You are filthy and disgusting. You make me sick!"

With this, the baby pauses, looks at the man, then points and starts laughing hysterically.

Babies are smart.

So I'm on a bus. There's a real battle of wits and perseverance between two gentlemen. There's a guy in his mid-forties who is opening the window, feeling that it's stuffy and that the bus could do with a refreshing breeze.

The younger guy in his early twenties, however, is closing the window behind him, possibly feeling that the draft is too cold.

It has gone back and forth eight times now. They've not said a word to each other.

I'm wondering who will break first. My money's on the older guy, who huffs each time he has to get back up to open it. The young lad is smiling every time he sits down after closing the window, revelling in the older man's misery.

I'm on the edge of my seat watching this fascinating psychological contest.

Although, I'm actually on the edge of my seat because it's my stop next.

38

So I'm on a bus. An empty can is rolling on the floor of the busy bus, rattling away. It's a classic dilemma. Pick it up and put it in the bin, or let it continue rattling in peace?

No one else has picked it up.

I decide to stay put. Mustn't make a scene. Can't let the rest of the bus know that a measly little can is getting to me. Noisy little bastard.

An old lady gets on the bus, spots the can, picks it up and puts it straight in the bin.

What a remarkable and fearless woman.

So I'm on a bus. It's incredibly hot, and it's kicking out time at the schools. The bus stops outside a school and proceeds to fill up with school kids. The bus is now packed. Grim.

Within minutes, the infuriating little degenerates have decided that they'll keep pressing the stop button as much as possible, sending the buzzer ringing through the bus. They think this is hilarious. I look around disapprovingly, but one of the more astute of the pack has clocked onto this and pressed the button even more. Cute.

The bus stops at the next stop. No one gets on, no one gets off. But the bus stays there for at least two minutes.

One of the creatures calmly shouts, "No one's getting off here, mate."

At this moment, the bus driver gets out of his seat, marches up the gangway and declares, "I'm waiting for twelve people to get off my bus. Who's it going to be?"

The school kids look back blankly.

"If you're going to take the piss, then get off my bus right now!" says the driver, who sits back down and starts the bus again.

It's my stop next. So I turn to the kids behind me, smile and proceed to press the button ten times. They look on in horror as I get up and head to the front of the bus. I turn to the driver and say, "That wasn't me by the way."

"Don't worry, son," he says, "They'll be chucked off in a minute."

Whoops.

So I'm on a bus. I ask the driver for my usual day pass, handing over £3.60 exactly.

"Sorry," she says, "that's gone up to £4."

"Oh, my bad. I didn't realise," I reply. I take back the change and hand her a £10 note.

"Do you have the right change?" she asks.

"I did have the right change, but you put the price up," I say.

She sighs, and then says, "I don't have the change for a £10 note. Do you not have the extra 40p?"

"I have an extra £13.60 in total. I had the correct change. If you're going to put the price up by ten percent, there's not much else I can do, right?"

42

She pauses briefly, and then says, "I'll let you off this once and take the £3.60. But normally I wouldn't be able to let you on."

"Let me off?" I say, as my ticket prints. "For having more than the required amount of money? That's mental! Surely you should be able to cater for giving change for £4 fares? That's not exactly loose change, right?"

She just looks at me, implying I need to sit down and shut up.

Are there any other businesses where you try and buy something, but are made to feel bad for not having the correct change? You wouldn't see this sort of thing happening in Tesco.

"Do you have the exact change for these groceries? No? Sorry, that's not good enough, you can't have them. Get out of my shop."

So I'm on a bus. Nothing causes more pandemonium than a wasp on a packed bus during the school run. The screaming. So much screaming.

44

So I'm on a bus. The mood is tense. It's unusually rammed for this time of day, with the elderly accounting for 90 percent of the passenger ratio. Standing at the back (I gave my seat to an elderly gentleman; it's the right thing to do) I look down the aisle and see one lady really kicking up a fuss.

There's a young man who's sitting in an elderly/disabled seat at the front with his headphones on. Rather than tap him on the shoulder and ask if she can have the seat, she's making sure the whole bus knows of this man's sheer ignorance. This lady really wants to moan about it.

"How dare he sit there when someone elderly like me needs a seat!" she barks, "The youth of today have no respect!" She sounds like an angry Daily Mail reader. She doesn't even look that old.

This continues for a few stops. Then the young man presses the button, bends down, picks up some crutches, and slowly prises himself out of his seat, with a badly broken foot quite clearly on display.

He calmly pulls his headphones down, looks at the lady and says, "This seat is free now. Sorry for the lack of respect."

He limps off the bus, and the lady sheepishly sits in the vacant seat. Red-faced.

So I'm on a bus. Some obnoxious brat of a kid is being a loud pain in the arse with his mates this morning, much to the annoyance of the other passengers. Hell-bent on showing off, he starts to throw a pocket Bible around (like you do). He then tries to throw the small book at another school pupil who the group has been taunting the entire journey. But he misses. The Bible hits me.

The kids laugh quietly but hysterically. I pick the Bible up off the floor. After a few minutes, the loud brat comes up to me and asks for it back.

"Sorry, lad – my Bible now."

He pleads with me that I need to give it back, otherwise he will get a detention in his religious education class. To which I reply, "You should have thought about that before you started throwing it at strangers on a bus."

Conveniently, it's my stop, so I get off the bus. With the kid looking on in dismay, I drop his Bible in the bin. Tough love.

So I'm at a bus stop. I'm standing at the back of a four-person queue. Nothing too crazy. At the front is an elderly lady, who must be in her eighties, with a Zimmer frame. She also has three bags of shopping. As the bus pulls up, she's clearly struggling to get on the bus with all her things. I quickly step up and help her with her bags so she can get herself and her Zimmer frame on the bus. I take her bags and follow her to her seat.

"Thank you, dear!" she chirps, as she sits down. As I go back to purchase my ticket, a middle-aged woman who was also in the queue looks at me sternly.

I gesture for her to go in front of me.

"I should think so too, pushing in front of me!" she snaps.

48

I say nothing, a bit shocked at this anger directed at me. I pay for my ticket and sit near the front.

As the bus pulls away, the middle-aged lady yells, "Stop! I've left my handbag at the bus stop!" and frantically scuttles to the bus driver. The bus driver stops the bus to let her off.

She turns to me and says, "This is your fault."

I reply, "I'm sorry, I didn't realize I'd made a mistake and helped the wrong lady with the task of getting her bags on the bus. I'll choose you next time seeing as you find it so tough!"

She huffs and leaves. Miserable old bat.

49

So I'm on a bus. There's an elderly couple sitting a few seats in front of me. They've just been to the doctors. I know this, as does the rest of the bus, because the old lady is reading the prescriptions and directions for use out loud.

"So you need to take this for your hemorrhoids. That's a lot of medicine! I still don't understand why they wouldn't change your willy cream if it isn't working!"

Wow.

So I'm on a bus. An old lady leaves her seat to get off. It's a fold-up seat, though, and as she stands up, the seat lifts her skirt up as the seat springs back, revealing everything.

I might get off a few stops early and make an appointment with the psychiatrist for the years of counselling I'm going to need to erase this image from my mind.

BUS	DESTINATION	TIME
35	The Green Mile	16:12

So I'm at a bus stop. Waiting for my bus. My stop is three stops from the start of the bus route. In the last 50 minutes, I've seen five buses go by in the opposite direction.

It would seem that the number 20 bus goes to Hullbridge town centre to die.

So I'm on a bus. I should not be this excited about the fact that the bus I'm on is brand spanking new. But here I am, appreciating every contour of this marvellous machine.

The usual smells of sweat, food stains and grime are replaced with fresh aromatic new plastic. No chewing gum embedded in the seats. Scratched graffiti on the windows non-existent. My seat is comfortable with plenty of legroom. What a treat!

I look around to see if others approve, sharing in my delight. But they don't care at all.

They're on a bus for goodness' sake.

So I'm on a bus. Some maniac in a Range Rover pulls out so fast in front of us that the driver pulls off the most ridiculous swerve to avoid a collision, and stops the bus safely.

No witty retort here. The bus driver is a bloody hero.

So I'm on a bus...

BUS	DESTINATION	TIME
38	David vs. Goliath	09:32

So I'm at a bus stop. It's a busy stop in the town centre, with nine different bus routes stopping here. It's quite busy at this time of day, with around twenty people waiting for buses.

Suddenly, a road sweeper appears. The man driving it has decided that now is a good time to sweep the pavement. As he moves towards us, he waits, gesturing that we need to move out of the way. The pavement is narrow, so I have to step into the main road onto the bus lane, pretty much into oncoming traffic. It's a bit bloody dangerous.

Everyone else in the waiting bus queues are forced to follow suit, grabbing their bags as the big metal machine of inconvenience trundles on, noisily spraying dirty water into their paths.

As the road sweeper nears the end of the bus stops, an old lady on a mobility scooter, wearing a bright pink coat, confronts him. Again, the road sweeper stops, and the driver gestures to her that she has to move.

This lady isn't going anywhere. We have a Mexican standoff.

The tiny mobility scooter is directly facing the huge road sweeper. This is an epic confrontation. The road sweeper really needs to get by. But this old lady refuses to be intimidated.

After about three minutes, the road sweeper man reluctantly gives up, and embarks on the tricky task of precariously reversing his machine all the way back the way he came.

It's impossible not to admire the cojones this old lady just showed. She slayed the giant.

So I'm on a bus...		
BUS DESTINATION		TIME
39 Fight Club		08:09

So I'm on a bus. I'm watching a schoolgirl kick seven shades of crap out of a schoolboy. I should probably intervene. But it is very funny. And I am very hungover.

So I'm at a bus stop. I've been waiting a while, so I'm playing a game on my smartphone while I wait for my bus.

Suddenly my bus appears, so I pause my game and quickly step on and ask for a day pass.

"You make our lives a bit harder when you're stuck to your bloody phones, glued to those bloody games," says the bus driver judgementally, while processing my ticket.

Sensing the strong undertone of smarminess in his voice, I reply, "Well you made my life a bit harder by deciding to turn up 19 minutes late rather than sticking to the timetable, but I chose to keep that to myself. Sorry."

So I'm on a bus. It's -5°C outside, but totally against the state of play, the bus is delightfully warm. It's so snug and cosy on here.

We're stuck in traffic but I couldn't care less. I look out my window and watch pedestrians fighting with the elements. School kids struggling to stay on their feet, their school bags making them top-heavy as they slide over the sheets of ice on the pavement floor. Commuters looking more miserable than usual, as their noses glow red in the face of icy winds. Elderly people appearing spherical with their eight layers of clothing. It's not a good day to be a pedestrian.

But I don't care. I'm on a bus.

I'm having a great time.

So I'm on a bus. Three teenage lads have just got on.

"Child single to Southend, please," says the first guy.

The bus driver looks at him and then says, "Can I see some proof of age, please? Otherwise I'm charging you full fare."

"Aw, I don't have any. I'm 15, though, honest."

The driver calmly replies, "The cigarette tucked behind your ear and the four-pack of cider in your carrier bag would suggest otherwise, son."

Mikey Glenister is a 30 year old musician from Southend-On-Sea, Essex.

Mikey has a decade of experience as a professional trumpeter and drummer under his belt, playing high profile acts such as 'Get Cape. Wear Cape. Fly'. Through his ten years playing with Get Cape, Mikey has made many TV appearances, including The Culture Show, and a cameo on UK soap opera 'Hollyoaks'.

Mikey does not own a car.

Lee Baker is a *40 something* cartoonist, graphic designer and creative retoucher from Essex.

He has been drawing cartoons and creating humour for nearly thirty years and has over twenty three years experience in the print and design industry.

Twelve years spent with legendary album cover designer Storm Thorgerson had Lee working for some of the biggest bands in the world including; Pink Floyd, Muse and Biffy Clyro to name a few.

He is the sole creative force behind *Yonks Ago!* – a series of illustrated fantasy novels for children about the zany adventures of a prehistoric tribe.

Unlike Mikey, he does own a car.

SO I'M ON A BUS

www.facebook.com/soimonabus